TEMPTATIONS

VOLUME 2

A collection of erotic stories

Edited by Miranda Forbes

Published by Accent Press Ltd – 2009
ISBN 9781907016295

Printed and bound in the UK

Cover design by
Red Dot Design

Contents

French Top-up
By Alicia Carter

'Very unusual name, Tissy,' François said, gently placing a cup of coffee in front of me. 'I've not heard that before.' His deep French tones were already sending shivers down my spine, making my body tingle all over. He smiled warmly as he took a sip from his cup.

'When I was really young, six or seven maybe,' I said, smiling appreciatively at my coffee, 'I started hating my real name – Sissy – which believe me, led to no end of teasing.' I leaned forward to pick up my cup, admittedly further forward than I needed to, just so I could offer him a good look down the top of my loose-fitting blouse. In the coffee table reflection I saw his expression change – he was staring straight down it! I lingered for a moment, absent-mindedly turning the cup handle, allowing him a longer peek at my breasts, which were completely exposed after removing my bra outside his apartment door.

I grasped my coffee cup and quickly sat up. Disappointment! Not even a touch of embarrassment on his face. I guess plenty of girls had flirted with him over the years – *but I'm more determined than any of them!* I slowly uncrossed my bare legs, allowing them to drift apart a few inches, pulling my short skirt perilously high on my lap.

'I tried Missy for a bit,' I continued, as if I *hadn't* just opened my legs for him, 'until I understood the *spoiled brat* connotation. Then I misheard a friend shouting Tissy, Tissy ... and I sort of liked it.'

He smiled warmly back at me, 'Very good, very good.' Up close, he was much more attractive than I'd expected. I'd seen him strolling around campus a few times, and had watched him *from the sidelines*, playing squash with a guy on my course. Now, sat here right in front of me, he looked absolutely gorgeous. I'd been told he was around 46, which made sense, as he exuded a lifetime's worth of confidence and experience. The elegant way he moved, and his smooth calm tones were very appealing. The fact that he'd maintained his dignity despite five minutes of concentrated flirting told me I had a real challenge on my hands – *time to pick things up a bit I think!*

'So an exchange, with Paris University for six

weeks, to study ...'

'... The Future of Modern Digital Media,' I replied proudly.

'Ah, very ... good.' He'd hesitated because I'd leant forward again to put my coffee cup down. Only this time I'd gone down *much* further, under the pretence of a problem with my shoe that I just had to sort.

'Sorry, an itch,' I lied. My blouse now hung low enough for him to take in the full shape of my breasts, and my painfully erect nipples. I shifted a few times, making my breasts wobble, keeping his eyes firmly glued to them.

'So I was looking to top-up my French a little before heading off,' I said, still apparently struggling with my shoe, pleased as punch his eyes were still staring down inside my blouse. Better still, I saw a generous-looking swelling grow in his trousers. The thought of reaching in and exposing his cock was making me wet between the legs.

'Will you do it for me?' I gasped, a little cheekily.

He snapped his head up quickly, and for the first time looked a little self-conscious. 'Of course I will ... do it for you.' I could see him wince at his own words.

'What shall we do first?' I said, keeping the suggestive talk going, and elegantly flicking back my long silky hair. He crossed his legs, seeming to be in some discomfort.

'We'll start simple,' he said quickly, clearly keen to get on with the tuition, to keep us both distracted. 'I'll shout out in English, and you translate ... en français. Oui?' I just nodded, feigning a nervous smile. He laughed back, trying to relax me a little – but I was more relaxed, more in control, than he could ever imagine.

'OK, here we go. Coffee.' His voice clear and commanding.

'Café ... easy.' I slapped my bare legs playfully.

'Decaffeinated coffee.'

'Café ... décaféiné?' The pause for pronunciation just for show.

'Good. OK. How about ... I have travellers' cheques?'

'Shit, I need to sort those,' I said to myself, genuinely irritated. 'Umm ... J'ai les chèques-voyage.'

'Excellent.' He seemed genuinely pleased with my pronunciations. 'OK, let's try out a few simple phrases.'

'Great, thanks,' I said enthusiastically, while reaching forward once more for my coffee cup. His expression dropped, and I'm sure his heart was racing in anticipation. I let him take in another

4

view of my naked breasts, but only for a moment this time, before sitting up straight. Then with my eyes locked to his, I brought the coffee cup up to my lips and drank deeply from it, allowing a little of the warm fluid to leak from my mouth and trail down my chin and neck. I arched my body right back as I emptied the cup, pushing my chest out towards him. With a hand around my back, I pulled the blouse material tight, so my naked breasts pressed hard against the thin material, stretching it rudely, showing off their delicious curves. My aching nipples poked hard against the cotton, showing him in no uncertain terms how turned on I was. I heard him gulp. For my *pièce de résistance*, while my body was arched right back, I allowed my legs to slowly drift steadily apart, revealing more and more of my milky-white inner thighs. As they parted, my skirt rode up to reveal – and I'm sure he must have nearly come in his pants at this – that I wasn't wearing any panties, *and* that I was completely shaven bar a tiny bit of hair shaved into a heart shape – which also resembled an arrow pointing straight down to my hot wet slit.

'I'm ready,' I purred suggestively, replacing the empty coffee cup, relishing the look of horror on his face. For a few moments, he was dumbstruck.

He was flustered, 'From what I've … heard

you say so far, I think you should be fine in Paris.' He glanced nervously at his watch, while his other hand fixed further discomfort in his trousers.

'Please,' I said innocently, closing my legs just a little bit, as if it had all been a misunderstanding on his part. 'I really need topping up.' His eyes flicked up and down my body as he desperately decided what to do.

'OK,' he said finally, having found some calm. 'What about a few simple phrases, Tissy?'

'That would be very useful, thanks, François.'

'Very good! Here we go,' he said quickly, indicating we were going to up the pace, probably to keep both of our minds on the job in hand. My mind already was!

'How are you?' he asked quickly.

'Comment allez-vous?'

'Where can I get some information?' His words were simple and direct, like a teacher's, which started a warm glow in my crotch.

'Où peux-je ... obtenir de l'information?'

'Is my train on time?' he asked, as if talking to someone at a station.

Tricky one this. 'Mon train a-t-il .... lieu à l'heure?'

'That's it, excellent, Tissy. Now,' he said, his voice taking on a much more serious tone, 'this is an extremely useful phrase.' He kept me waiting

6

for a moment, then said, 'How much is a beer?' After a tiny pause, he laughed at himself a little under his breath.

'Combien coûte une bière?' I laughed back, keeping the mood light.

'How much for two beers?' he shot straight back.

'Combien pour deux bières. Easy peasy lemon *squeezy*.' I lifted the stakes again, by idly scratching at a nipple, as if it were bugging me. When it hardened further under my touch, I wanted to play with it more. I pictured myself pinching and squeezing it through my blouse, maybe even wetting my fingers and thumbs so when I worked it some more, the material turned transparent ... but I didn't, not yet. His eyes followed every move of my finger as it scratched away. He noticed me observing him, and quickly jerked his head up.

'I am looking for the university,' he choked finally, the words becoming a struggle now.

'Je cherche l'université.' I spoke clearly and confidently this time, leaving no trace of the uncertainty I'd faked earlier. *Time to move in for the kill!*

'Excuse me, where is the restaurant?' His forehead was coated with a thin sheen of sweat, and he was shifting uncomfortably in his seat.

'Excusez-moi, où est le restaurant?' I said ever so slowly and sexily, while sliding forward on my chair and opening my legs wider, this time completely exposing my naked crotch to his gaze. While he was struggling to form the next line in his head, I leant forward once more, so he could see my breasts again. Now his gawping eyes were torn between my heaving breasts and hot wet pussy. I slipped a hand down to my inner thigh, where I idly stroked a few fingertips on my soft flesh, slowly circling closer and closer to my crotch.

'I would like to go to my bedroom,' he spat quickly, just to say something, doing his best to keep his eyes locked to my face. Then a look of horror at what he'd said. I smiled back simply at his embarrassment and licked my tongue slowly around my lips, wetting them. Now he didn't know where to look.

'Je voudrais aller à ma chambre à coucher,' I replied sexily, drawing out every word, as I started leaning right over the coffee table towards him.

'I would like some decaffeinated coffee please,' he mumbled, desperately trying to change the subject.

'Je voudrais du café décaféiné svp.'

'I would like some help please.' From his expression, he really did.

'Je voudrais de l'aide svp,' I said perfectly, every subtlety and nuance nailed. *Then I turned the tables!*

'Now it's my turn,' I purred sexily, stepping over the coffee table to stand straddling his legs. 'You translate what *I'm* saying, François.' Just saying his name made my pussy throb deliciously – in anticipation at what we were about to do.

'Je voudrais,' I said, watching him staring at my lips, 'enlever mes vêtements.' I felt like a goddess standing over him – immensely powerful, and full of sexual energy.

'You, err ... I mean *I*,' he gasped, 'would like to ... take my clothes off?' His eyes flitted up and down my body like a schoolboy's, taking in all my features, close up. I pulled out the bottom of my loose-fitting blouse, allowing him to look up inside, at my heaving breasts, which were now within his reach. I saw his lips moisten at the prospect.

'Je voudrais votre robinet,' I said lustfully, stroking a finger along the length of the bulge in his trousers.

'I would like your ... cock?' he translated, overcome with emotion, but not halting my teasing his digit. I smiled affirmation, then leaned in really close, so my lips were inches from his face. He licked his lips nervously.

9

'J'ai besoin de votre robinet.' He was shocked. I'd asked him to translate *I need your cock* – which I did, *right away!* I reached down and unzipped his fly, then expertly pulled out his cock. He did nothing to stop me, as if paralysed. François' cock was as beautiful as I'd imagined, long and thick. I moved my wanting mouth close to his, and flicked my tongue across his lips, wetting them.

'You are very beautiful,' he gasped, his warm breath washing over me, making me more gooey inside. 'Vous êtes très belle,' he repeated, this time in his native tongue.

I pressed my lips against his. 'Embrassez-moi,' I said, into his mouth. He did and kissed me delicately at first, then with growing, unrestrained passion. I tilted his head gently with my fingers and kissed him harder, pushing my tongue through his lips, squeezing them apart, tasting the inside of his mouth. I squatted lower, until my wet naked pussy pressed down against his stiff cock. It slipped naturally into position along my pussy, pressing my engorged lips apart, which by now were completely coated in my juices. I rocked back and fore on it, sliding along its length, but not letting him in. He was breathing hard into my mouth as we continued kissing. Suddenly, he pulled his mouth away.

'Baisez-moi,' he gasped, bucking his hips,

sliding his cock rhythmically along the outside of my wet slit, the head sometimes rubbing deliciously across my swollen clit.

'Oh I do want you to *fuck me*, François,' I said, flashing my tongue quickly across the lips of his gaping mouth. 'But we don't need to rush.'

He pulled my lips to his, slipping his tongue inside my mouth, his cock still sliding effortlessly along my sopping crotch as he did. I closed my eyes for a moment, delighting in the deep guttural heat growing in my belly that would soon build to an almighty climax.

François' hands were at my breasts now, groping them through my blouse, pinching masterfully at my nipples through the flimsy material. I wanted him to rip my blouse free, carelessly tearing the delicate material apart, and popping the buttons, sending them pinging across the room. He didn't ... *so I did!* I cast the ripped blouse behind me, and immediately François' mouth latched on to a breast, sucking greedily at the nipple, rolling his tongue around it, which instantly drove me wild. Suddenly he pulled his sucking lips free, and locked on to my other breast, immediately slurping away with relish, pulling my breast flesh deeper into his mouth, then lashing at my sensitive nipple with the stiff tip of his tongue. I groaned deeply, letting my head fall back, as I

11

continued riding his cock, sliding my soaking pussy along it, while he feasted on my breasts.

His mouth was on the move again, his tender lips kissing steadily upwards, leaving a warm wet trail, until they settled on my exposed neck. He nibbled and sucked lightly all around it. God he was good. I loved a man lavishing attention on my neck. He kissed and licked excitedly, leaving trails of saliva as his mouth moved to suck on the other side of my neck. I angled my head the other way to give him more access. I wanted this to last forever!

Still lovingly attending to my neck, and then my mouth, he slipped his hands under my thighs and lifted me up, his hands strong and firm. He positioned the tip of his cock at my now gaping hole, but tantalisingly held it there for a moment, just poised at the sopping entrance – maybe to tease me, or to wait for permission. I wanted it. By now, I *needed* it! Slowly, I lowered myself down the full length of his cock, until it was all the way inside me, right up to the hilt. God it felt great. I could feel his cock throb and swell inside me, filling me completely. He shifted his grip in readiness to fuck me. I needed to hold off a just a little longer. I leaned back, reluctantly pulling my neck from his wondrous lips.

'Ah, ah, ah,' I chastised breathlessly, waving a finger at him as if he were a naughty boy. 'Not yet,

François ... not yet!' While still straddling his lap, with his thick cock still twitching deep inside me, I pushed out my chest, shamelessly presenting my breasts to his hands and mouth once again. I felt his cock twitch, and grow even longer inside me as he took in the sight of my breasts, still wet and shiny from his sucking earlier.

'Sucez mes seins,' I ordered, pushing a breast at his mouth. He lunged forward to meet it, instantly sucking on my tender flesh. His lips closing on my nipple was like bolt of electricity, sending out a surge of sexual energy all around my body, making my pussy pulse around his cock.

'Oh, fuck,' I gasped, letting my head fall back as he sucked deeply on my breast flesh, pulling it deep into my mouth, then sliding it out and nipping gently at my nipple, driving me wild. 'That is so ... good.' I pulled my breast free, and urgently fed him the other one. He sucked and slurped noisily on it, exactly as I desired. He bit a little harder on my delicate bud, making me groan out loud, and then dragged his lips to the other breast to do the same.

'Yes, suck it!' I groaned, looking down at his lips greedily feeding on my breast, 'suck it, suck it hard!' He pushed a flat tongue around my breast, licking it all over, covering it with his saliva. As he did, I felt his hips slowly bucking, ever so lightly

13

starting to fuck me. I went with it, allowing him to ease his cock out an inch more, and then I took control, and dropped back down his length until he was completely inside me again. We slipped into a slow, steady rhythm, our bodies beginning to move as one. I pulled his mouth up to mine, his lips warm and wet. We kissed like long-lost lovers.

I started sliding up his cock a little further each time, then dropping harder and faster back down it, making him gasp into my mouth. Our tongues twisted and battled deep in our mouths, while I bobbed quicker and quicker on his cock.

'Baisez-moi!' This time *I* told him to fuck *me*. And I needed it now, hard and fast. He forced his cock hard upwards, at exactly the same time I dropped hard down on it. I braced my hands on the back of his chair to steady myself, as I energetically fucked him, relishing each time he plunged deep inside my soaking wet pussy. My orgasm was building fast. I was leaking all over his cock.

'Rapide,' I grunted, urging him to fuck me faster. 'François – rapide!'

'Oh Tissy … vous êtes un slut… God, you are the best … vous m'avez attrapé,' he muttered. He was moments away now.

I felt his hands squeezing at my breasts as I clamped my lips to his, lustfully sliding my tongue around the inside of his mouth. He pulled roughly at my nipples, and squeezed them hard between his fingers and thumbs, making me moan into his lips. I felt my body convulse, my pussy pulsing wildly around his cock. I could feel his muscles tense. My pussy was on fire now. I reached down, and desperately frigged my clit as his energetic thrusts started pounding deeper and deeper into me.

'I'm coming,' he shouted. I slipped off his cock and wedged it against my sopping pussy, wanking him along my slit, using his throbbing cock as a dildo. My hand was a blur, sliding quickly and easily along the length of his juice-soaked cock. I pressed myself hard against it, my fingers brushing deliciously against my twitching clit with each stroke. He started licking roughly at my nipples, which took me over the edge, and triggered my orgasm. Flashes of heat washed over me, making me twist and writhe on his lap, sending sparks of ecstasy through my whole body, making me shake uncontrollably. He exploded simultaneously, his sperm jetting out over his belly, across my hand and then, when I pulled the still stiff flesh tighter towards me, all over my flat tummy. I held it there as it finished twitching, enjoying the feel of the big throbbing flesh as it pulsed in my hand.

We were both breathing hard, chests heaving,

when I leaned in and whispered into his ear. 'Thank you for my lesson, François.' Then I gave his ear a cheeky lick.

He gave me a firm kiss on the lips, then eased my head away. 'You didn't really have any problems with your French, did you?'

I smiled sweetly. 'Let's just say I had a degree of confidence coming here tonight,' and I leaned in and kissed him one more time.

As I stepped out of the door, he said something that left me puzzled, and extremely curious. He told me I ought to do a little research on the name Tissy, because he was sure he'd heard it before somewhere. Then bizarrely, he'd laughed to himself, and made some comment about it being oddly appropriate. As I strolled away, still with a grin on my face like the cat that's got the cream, I decided I'd Google it as soon as I got home.

Getting the Cane
by Roxanne Sinclair

Sarah indicated left and waited for a gap in the traffic. She was still in two minds about going through the gates. When she had walked away from here ten years before she had vowed never to return, yet here she was, and she still hadn't worked out why.

She pulled the car into one of the few empty spaces that were left. She turned off the engine and looked at the building in front of her.

Her old school looked just the way that it always had, dull and drab.

This was a mistake, she decided, and was just about to start the engine so that she could get the hell out of here when she was startled by a knock on the driver's window.

The face of a wide-eyed woman with a freakish smile was inches away from her own. Thank God for glass, Sarah thought. Suddenly the door was pulled open and there was nothing to protect her from the person who Sarah couldn't place but who did look vaguely familiar.

'Sarah Patterson,' the woman shrieked, 'as I live and breathe.'

Then she had it. 'Maggie,' Sarah said as she was pulled out of the car. 'Lovely to see you again,' she lied.

'You haven't changed a bit.' Maggie allowed Sarah just enough time to lock the car door before pulling her towards the building.

'You look just the same too,' Sarah lied again, adding the words 'apart from about four stones' in her head.

Seconds later Maggie had latched on to some other poor sap who was having second thoughts and Sarah almost took the opportunity to hotfoot it in the opposite direction. But she was here now, she finally conceded, so she decided that she might as well go in and show her face. She had nothing else to do.

After twenty minutes of mingling among the class of '99 she remembered why she hadn't kept in touch with any of them. They hadn't been her friends then and she had no desire to make them her friends now.

She didn't know whose idea this ten-year reunion had been but it had been a bloody stupid one. She made a mental note to bin the invitation to the next one.

She didn't bother telling anyone that she was leaving, she just did.

She was the only person in the corridor and her heels echoed as she walked.

She was almost out of the place when something caught her attention. Through the glass panel of the door on her right she saw him, the only reason that she had gone to school during that last year.

It had been the History Room when she was at school and she guessed that it still was unless he had started teaching something else. She could only see his back as he stood at the board writing, but she had stared at him doing that for seven hours a week during the last two years of her school life and she knew it was him. She wondered if he still looked the same from the front.

There was only one way to find out.

But could she do it? She remembered the way he'd made her feel and what she'd wanted him to do to her. Seeing him again she still wanted him to do those things. She knew what might happen if she went into that room.

She knocked on the glass panel of the door and opened it.

'Yes,' he said, without turning around.

He sounded the same and Sarah tingled with

the anticipation of again seeing the face that had tormented her dreams for over two years.

'Mr Watts,' she said, once again feeling like the nervous schoolgirl who had been sent to give a message to the teacher with the incredible eyes. It was when she'd looked into those eyes for the first time that she'd decided History was the subject for her in Sixth Form.

He looked over his shoulder and looked at her. Even at this distance she could tell that those eyes were as vibrant as ever.

'Hello, Mr Watts,' she said, feeling ever so slightly foolish.

'Sarah Patterson.' He said her name as he turned around to face her.

He remembered her.

'That's me.' She tried but probably failed to sound jovial.

'You look great,' he said, taking her in from top to bottom. When his eyes lingered on the top a little longer than was necessary, Sarah almost came on the spot.

Then his eyes met hers. 'So do you,' she said.

And still they looked at each other.

'You haven't changed at all,' he managed to say eventually.

A smile split her face. She took a deep breath. Here goes. 'Oh no, sir,' she purred, 'that's where you're wrong.'

'Really?' he looked confused.

She took a couple of steps towards him and announced. 'I'm not your pupil anymore.' She hoped that he knew what she meant because she didn't think she would have the courage to offer it again.

He nodded his head slightly. Ten years ago Sarah had been a pretty young girl with a crush on him. Now she stood before him a gorgeous young woman with something else on her mind, and he thought he knew what it was.

When she grabbed hold of his shirt, pulled him towards her and planted her lips on his he knew that they were on the same wavelength.

Her kiss was hungry and intense, her lips soft and sweet.

When she looked at him under her long, dark lashes and smiled in that way that she always used to, he remembered why he wanted to fuck her. He recalled how on more than one occasion he had to sit at his desk longer than he wanted to hide the hard cock that his trousers struggled to disguise.

What had he been supposed to do? Her tits had been big, her blouses had been tight and they were always opened to the third button, which allowed a more than adequate glimpse of cleavage.

It was there and it was on view. It would have

21

been rude not to look. And he had looked and he had become rock hard.

He was just as hard now.

Her tits were still big and her blouse was still tight. They looked even better close up.

She placed a hand on each of his ears and laced her fingers into his hair. She pulled his face deep into her chest. And she laughed.

She was still laughing when she lifted his head and looked into his eyes.

When they had last been in this classroom he had had to be the one in control, the teacher authority figure who had been forced to fight the urge to lift her on to the desk and shag her. Now she was the one in charge, but that was OK because he knew that he would do whatever she told him to.

He watched her walk towards the door, not thinking for a second that she was going to walk through it. She didn't disappoint him.

She pulled down the blind to cover the glass panel and set a chair against the handle.

She didn't want an audience.

Then her hands were in front of her and by the time she turned to face him again her blouse was open and her tits sat pert and proud inside a baby blue bra. They were magnificent orbs that were barely contained within the straining lace and bounced up and down as she walked slowly and purposefully back to where he stood.

At last he didn't have to worry about that stalk that she had caused. He couldn't have hid it even if he had wanted to, which he didn't. He wanted Sarah to see the effect that she had on him, the effect that she had always had on him.

She had already seen it and by the look on her face she was having some of it.

With a tilt of her head and a smile on her face, she asked. 'Sir, is that your cane?'

'Yes.'

She didn't take her eyes from his as she worked the button and unzipped his trousers. She lowered his trousers and underpants to his knees, taking the opportunity to kiss the end of his cock. The clothes fell to his ankles and he stepped out of them.

'Are you going to give me your cane, sir?' she asked.

'That depends. Have you been bad, Miss Patterson?'

'I could be,' she laughed.

'Then yes, Miss Patterson, you will feel the length of my cane.'

Sarah moved towards him again and forced him back until he hit the board that he had been writing on. Then she pushed herself against him, forcing her breasts against his chest.

Once more her lips searched out his and he welcomed them. He felt her tongue inside his mouth and he responded with his own.

He peeled Sarah's blouse from her shoulders and freed her breasts from her bra with a single swift movement. He took a mound in each hand and used circular movements to knead them. Moments later his mouth covered one of her nipples and he sucked hard.

She moaned her encouragement and he sucked harder.

And as he sucked he pushed his hands under her skirt and searched out the promised land of her pussy.

Once inside her knickers he used his fingers to open her. Slowly he pushed his middle and forefinger into her moist hole. In and out he moved them, over and over again.

Then he released the breast that he had been chewing and pushed the fingers that had been deep inside her into his mouth and licked her juices from them.

'You could drink from the well if you like, sir,' she said, resting against the edge of the teacher's desk. She lifted her skirt and he saw that her knickers matched the bra that now sat on one of the desks in the front row.

Seconds later the knickers were on the same desk.

He traced her slit with the tip of his finger, delving slightly deeper with each pass until she opened.

He spread her lips and held them apart while he looked at her. He saw her clit twitching with anticipation.

He didn't keep her waiting. He used the tip of his tongue to flick her clitoris as he used his thumbs to massage the edge of her hole.

Within minutes she was dripping, and she begged him to work her harder. Seconds later she had another demand.

'Fuck me, sir.'

He didn't need asking twice.

He pushed his throbbing cock down from its vertical position and entered her easily. He pushed all the way in before he paused and savoured the moment. She wrapped her legs around him and held him in position. She put her hands behind her to take her weight and waited for him to go to work.

He started to move inside her, slowly at first, but increasing in speed with each thrust. Every time he entered her, her tits moved in time with his movements.

She shifted her weight onto one hand, freeing

the other to go to her clitoris, which she rubbed viciously, enhancing the pleasure that she was already feeling.

He meanwhile grabbed her hips and pulled her to him, grinding his groin into hers over and over again.

As he heard her moans grow louder he moved into her quicker and deeper, causing her breath to catch in her throat. The noise that came out as a tiny squeal fell into a rhythm of its own.

He felt her tightening around him, but her moisture meant that he could still slip in and out of her easily.

As his own pleasure intensified, so did the speed and ferocity of his thrusts. His thighs bounced off the edge of the desk that she was sitting on, but he wasn't thinking about the bruises that would be there by this time tomorrow, or how he was going to explain them to his wife.

As she gave in to the pleasure that she was feeling, she let out a deep moan.

'Fucking hell, Mr Watts,' she said through the deep breaths that followed her orgasm.

'Language, Miss Patterson,' he laughed.

She lay flat on the desk with her arms spread out and her fingers making grasping movements. Her eyes were closed and there was a broad grin on her face.

He continued to pummel her, but not for much longer.

The sight of her tight, hard little nipples moving in time with the tune that he was playing affected him more than he anticipated and he felt the juices in his balls heating up.

He knew that he would be filling her up very soon.

He put the palms of his hands on the desk to take his weight and banged into her hard, forcing another squeal from her with each penetration.

When he came, he came big, and he shuddered as it exploded out of him.

Finally spent, he rested against her. Her eyes were still closed and she was still smiling. Eventually her eyes opened and she chewed her lower lip as if she was thinking about something.

'What?' he asked.

'Sir,' she said, 'you just did a bad thing.'

'You were a very bad girl,' he told her. 'As I recall you didn't hand in the last piece of homework that I set you.'

She ignored the truth that he had spoken and told him, 'But it was very good.'

'And so were you.'

She stretched her neck until their lips connected. He rested his weight on his elbows and supported her weight with his hands under her arched back.

Then he kissed her back, hard.

He felt himself fall out of her as the angle he was leaning at changed.

They both took it as a sign that the moment was over.

He pushed himself upright and raised his boxer shorts over his soggy dick.

They dressed without sharing a word or a look. Oddly though, they were both thinking the same thing and that was that they had finally done something that they first dreamed of a decade earlier.

'Thank you for coming to see me, Miss Patterson,' he said as she stood with the open door in her hand.

'Not a problem, Mr Watts,' she said. 'If I'd known this was what happened when you didn't hand your homework in, I'd have done it more often.'

She closed the door behind her.

Knuckling Under
by Shanna Germain

Fingers. They do me in every time. Not eyes or a smile, not shoulders or calves, but fingers. I could be such a good girl, could keep my libido where it belongs, if it weren't for those fingers, promising to work their magic.

That time, it was my bike mechanic's fingers that I was lusting for. His fingers were big and long, muscular somehow. Each one was squared off at the tips with big, flat nails. Bits of bicycle grease filled the whirls of his knuckles and lined the edges of his fingernails.

The rest of him wasn't bad either: big chocolate eyes that I noticed right off. And then that just-long-enough curly dark hair. He had the body of a cyclist, lean and muscular in his jeans and blue T-shirt.

But there are lots of men who look like that. I'd resisted them. I thought I could resist him. He could have been just a pleasant daydream as I stood in line, my bike leaning on my hip, waiting for the woman in front of me to finish. He didn't raise his eyes much, and it gave me a chance to watch him, to imagine what it would be like to seduce him, to take him home. Just a dream, a way to pass the time.

I'd gotten pretty far in my daydream – to the point where he had hiked up my short work skirt and was running one finger up the inside of my thigh – by the time it was my turn. I stepped up to the counter with my bike in tow.

Nice smile, but shy. He didn't say anything, which he could only pull off because he was so adorable. He didn't even really take his eyes off my bike. You could tell he was more comfortable with bikes than people. But at least he didn't notice that I was wheeling my bike in while dressed in heels and my office ensemble while everyone else was sporting their padded bike shorts and super-fabric shirts. I'd had a hell of a time getting it out of the car, trying not to ruin my stockings since I had to go back to work.

'I have a flat,' I said.

I was kind of embarrassed to admit that I'd brought my bike to the shop for a flat tyre, but the truth is I'm not a bike geek. I like to ride, but I don't really understand how bikes work. I can't change my own tyre. I'd been telling myself that I was going to take a class and learn the basics. He'd just shot my incentive all to hell.

He motioned toward one of the rails behind the counter. 'Why don't you bring it round back?' he said.

I wheeled my bike around the edge of the counter. He took it from me and put it up on the rails. And that's when I saw his fingers, really saw them, for the first time. All that grease. A certain strength in the knuckles that comes from working with your hands. But his skin wasn't cut or chapped, and the grease was new. Like he went home every night and washed every bit of work from his hands, took care of them. It was that combination that got me. My light crush turned into a full-out throb that beat steady inside my underwear.

He caressed the curves of my bike with the pads of his fingers. My skin ached with longing. For once, I was jealous of my bike – I wanted those fingers on me, not on her.

'Nice bike,' he said.

She *was* a nice bike. Specialised, all white, unisex frame. A gift from my husband, who'd named her the White Goose. He called me Saraswathi, after the Hindu goddess of wisdom who rides a white goose, so it seemed appropriate. Only Saraswathi is supposed to represent purity itself. And here I was, doing – or dreaming of doing – just the opposite.

He ran those perfect fingers along the bike's curves and let them linger in her hidden spots. He pressed his fingers in the gear spots where she always wanted more oil, tucked them into the corner of the stem that always collected dirt. I'd always wanted a man like that, who could discover my hidden places and know intuitively how I wanted, needed, to be touched. Not sex, but something else. A discovery maybe. Or the feeling that someone knows you better than yourself.

Watching his fingers made me dizzy. The smooth sound of his skin sliding over her frame, the way he tucked his fingertips beneath the lip of the seat – it was too much. Then he moved down to the flat tyre. While he spun the wheel with one hand, he kept two fingers pressed to the side of the wheel. The sound was a steady slide, like someone pulling a skirt up over stockinged thighs.

'Aha,' he said. 'Here's your problem.'

When he hit the blow-out spot, he dug in, pulling the cut bit of tyre open. I wanted his fingers on me like that, sliding across me, opening me up.

'Looks like you hit a nice chunk of glass,' he said. He held out a triangle-shaped piece of green glass as though he were offering it to me. Its sharp

32

edges made his fingers look dangerous. 'The tyre should be okay, but you'll need a new tube.'

He dropped the glass on the counter and picked up a long black tool. The way his fingers moulded around the handle made the tool an extension of his hand. I wondered if you could learn a body like that, or if it was part of you. Every movement, every touch, more instinct than thought. He brought the tool toward my tyre, and then seemed to realise I was still standing there, watching.

'It'll only take me a couple of minutes. You can wait if you want to.'

I said something witty like, 'Could you tell me where the restroom is?' and then backed away, trying to pretend I wasn't still looking at his fingers.

In the employee restroom, I talked to the mirror. 'You will not do this,' I told my reflection. My reflection listened and nodded. Always the good girl. But my reflection's eyes were alive, shining in a way that she couldn't hide. And that corner of her lip, tilted up. I knew that neither of us was listening to my little speech.

I kept going anyway. I listed all the ways my husband was a good man: sexy, kind, put up with all of my shit. I didn't let myself think about his

33

hands. He had long, thin fingers. Soft as kid gloves. When he touched me, it was with long, soft strokes, like I was made of marzipan. Even when he put his fingers inside me, it was never more than two, never enough to stretch my body open. His fingers soothed, aroused. But never pressed, never opened me as far as I wanted him to. Never bruised.

I could resist this man. I would. And besides, he hadn't even noticed me. Didn't notice anything except my bike. Wasn't interested in me. At all.

It was this realisation that allowed me to grasp the doorknob to let myself out of the restroom. If I couldn't resist of my own accord, I would let his lack of interest do it for me. I would take my bike and go back to work. And tonight I would ride, pressing myself hard against the seat, thinking of his fingers.

I opened the door and stepped out, and there he was. Leaning against the hall wall, looking down at his shoes. His hands were tucked in his apron pockets. Without his fingers, he was avoidable. That's what allowed me to smile. To say something sharp and witty like, 'Oh, sorry, I didn't know you were waiting.'

He took his hands from his apron pockets and used them to push back his dark curls. One snagged on the meat of his finger, refusing to let go. It gave me a glimpse of how it would be to look down and see his finger wrapping itself in my own dark curls.

I tried to swallow or look away, but my muscles refused to obey. Every part of my body wanted to lean toward him like a magnet. I had one hand still on the doorknob. I don't know where my other hand was.

He looked up at me for the first time, those big brown eyes deep pools in his face.

'It's your calves,' he said.

My hand on the doorknob was doing a weird twisty thing that I couldn't seem to control. 'I'm sorry?' I said.

His fingers drifted back to his hair, pulling at a curl.

'I have a girlfriend, so I tried not to look,' he said. 'Tried not to, but I couldn't help it …'

His voice trailed away and he bit his lower lip with his two top teeth. Perfect squares against the pink flesh. When he looked back down, I realised he hadn't been looking at the floor or my bike all this time. He'd been looking at my legs.

I knew then that I wasn't the only one with a fetish, and that realisation allowed me to feel strong. I lifted my head – I would slip by him, let him into the bathroom and let myself out the front door. I would pay whoever needed to be paid and

I'd find another bike mechanic, a fat, ugly one with stubby little fingers.

As I moved, he put one finger out, like he was going to press an elevator button. I don't know if he meant to push the door open. Or maybe he meant to touch me on the shoulder. Either way, his finger ended up against my bottom lip. I tasted metal and grease and skin. I wanted to suck his finger into my mouth, to feel his calluses between my teeth. My tongue ran over the tip. The contrast between the smooth nail and the bits of rough skin at the edges took away the last of my resolve.

I sucked his finger into my mouth, held it there. He made a sound in the back of his throat, a low hum that made my belly contract. Keeping my lips tight around his finger, I led him backward into the restroom.

He let me lead him like that, and the door shut behind us, closing us into the small space. I let go of his finger, and he reached behind him to lock the door. His hands – fast and hard on my ass, on my thighs – and before I could even register it, he was lifting me up, setting me on the edge of the sink.

My skirt and his fingers made slippery sounds as he pushed the fabric up until my thighs were exposed. He put his hands between my legs, opened them until he could fit his body between.

I didn't know how to tell him what I wanted. It wasn't sex. It was those hands, those fingers.

Maybe he already knew. Maybe he'd realised my fetish when I'd sucked his finger into his mouth, because he put one hand up, smeared it roughly across my mouth like he was wiping away old lipstick. I caught one finger between my teeth on the way by, but he shook free, and closed his fingers around my chin. He tilted my head down, made me watch as he used his other hand to press into my thighs, to scratch at my stockings until small runs appeared.

He let go of my chin, but I could stand watching. His fingers made a small tear in the fabric, and then another, longer. Where he'd made the hole, his warm skin brushed mine. He burrowed his fingers beneath the fabric. I loved the way his hands looked, trapped under the see-through black, pressing hard into my skin.

His fingers grabbed the centre of my thong and pushed it aside. And then his fingers wrapped themselves in my curls, twisting and tugging. The contrast of my dark hair to his skin made it hard to breathe. Without waiting, he put his fingers inside me. Hard. Just like I'd hoped. I couldn't tell how many — two at least, maybe three. I was already wet, but the feel of his calluses lightly scratching the inside of me made me wetter.

He thrust his fingers into me, using his whole body, shoving my hips back and forth across the porcelain. I wrapped my calves around his back, and he made that low hum again in the back of his throat.

I couldn't watch any more. The feeling of it made me want to come, but watching his fingers fuck me was throwing me over the edge. I didn't want to come yet, so I closed my eyes and leaned back against the mirror. My reflection had turned her back on me, but I didn't care any more. I just wanted him to keep touching me the way he was doing.

'Watch,' he said, his voice low. It was a whisper, but it was also a command. I opened my eyes.

He took his fingers out of me and ran them, wet and glistening, down the inside of my thigh. Then he folded his hand, four fingers forming a point, and entered me once more. I watched as he pushed, slow but not gentle, inside me. He found my clit with his thumb, rubbed it hard enough to make me cry out, and then flicked at it with a fingernail. It was one second of pain and three of pleasure. And then it was all pleasure: watching his fingers move in and out of me, feeling the sharp edge of his thumb flicking in time to his strokes.

He reached back and wrapped his free hand around my calf muscle. His fingers dug in, and I tightened my legs around his back, made my calf muscles taut.

'Put your legs up,' he said, ducking down a little, his fingers never stopping their steady movement. I put my legs over his shoulders. The lip of the sink dug into my back, but I could barely feel it. All my nerve endings were working overtime around his fingers. There wasn't room to feel anything else.

'Tighter,' he said. I flexed my calves against his neck muscles. I wanted to reach down and touch him, to help him get off, but he seemed as focused on my calves as I was on his fingers, and I thought maybe he didn't want anything else.

He curled his fingers inside me – *come hither* – once, twice, against my G-spot, and I didn't think any more. I just closed my eyes and focused on his touch. Thumb flicking my clit. Fingertips hitting that sponge spot that made my body feel all shivery, shimmery.

My orgasm was as fast and hard as his fingers, rushing through me and then gone. He kept his fingers in, let me spasm around him until my body was still.

When he removed his fingers I felt empty, split open. I took my legs off his shoulders, surprised at how heavy they felt, how tired I was. The whole room smelled like grease and salt. I realised he was still dressed, that I'd hardly touched him. That he hadn't come.

I reached for his zipper, but he stopped my hands. His fingers were still wet from me.

'It's OK,' he said. He put one finger on my ripped stocking and ran it down to my calf. It left a glistening trail on the black. 'I got just what I wanted. Plus, I have to go back and finish your bike.'

I'd forgotten about the bike. Actually, for three or five or ten minutes, I'd forgotten about everything. Now, watching him reach for a paper towel to dry his fingers, it all came back. My promise to be a good girl. To keep my libido in check. To be true to my husband.

But you can't help what you love. Or what you lust after. And those fingers, those strong, sexy fingers, they get me every time.

Posh Boy
by Lucy Felthouse

I've always been a sucker for posh accents. I think it's because they tend to be associated with well-educated young men who are polite, gentlemanly … and just waiting to be corrupted. That's where I come in.

One of my favourite fantasies has always been to fuck a posh boy, just to hear him say dirty words in his sexy accent. Unfortunately, living up north, there aren't that many of them around. So it was a fantasy that lay dormant. That is, until Nathan came along.

I met him through a friend. Well, I say 'met', but it was all done over the telephone. It was my friend's birthday and I'd called him up to wish him a happy birthday. He and his mates were already drunk and boys will be boys – they all started yelling down the phone, thinking I was Nick's girlfriend. One voice in particular stood out. The words were out of my mouth before I could stop them – "Who was that, Nick?"

"Who?" he shouted over the din, "There's loads of us here."

"The last one. With the posh accent."

"Oh," said Nick, obviously remembering my penchant, confessed during a drunken night in the flat we used to share, "that's Nathan. Why, do you want to talk to him?"

"Is he single?"

"Find out for yourself."

I heard shuffling and laughter in the background. Then suddenly, "Hello?"

My heart began to thud and I felt a warmth between my thighs. Wow, I'd forgotten how much those accents got to me.

"Hi, Nathan."

"Nick said you wanted to talk to me." It had gone quiet now. The other guys were either so intent on listening that they'd shut up, or he was now alone.

"Yes," I wondered what to say, then decided that I'd probably never lay eyes on this guy, so it didn't matter, "I just thought you had a nice voice, that was all. A sexy accent."

"Thank you. So do you."

I giggled. "Yeah, right."

"No, really. It's got a lovely lilt to it. In fact I reckon I could listen to you all day."

And that's where it began. Nathan and I exchanged phone numbers and started chatting regularly. We had lots in common with books, films and our love of the outdoors so we were always laughing and talking rubbish, and got to know each other really quickly. Soon, the talk turned dirty. We were both single and bemoaned the lack of sex. There'd been no talk of meeting up, so I felt free to let rip with my wildest thoughts and fantasies. It wasn't doing anybody any harm, so I just enjoyed it.

One evening we were having a conversation and I asked how his day had been. His response wasn't entirely what I'd been expecting.

"Well, the guy upstairs has been shagging his missus. They've been at it like rabbits for ages and, frankly, I'm jealous and as horny as fuck."

I laughed out loud.

"Sorry, old fruit (yes, he really said that!), was I a bit too honest there?"

"No, it just wasn't what I was expecting you to say, that's all."

"Sorry. It has been a while though."

"Well then," I replied, feeling the same way myself, "you need to get laid then, don't you?"

"I do. I just wish you didn't live so far away."

"Me too. I'm sure we'd have a great time together."

"Oh, we would. I'd show you what you've been missing. Those idiot blokes round your way clearly haven't got a clue."

"Really?" I said, knowing exactly where this was going, "And how would you do that then?"

"I'd lick you and make you come until you ache, then fuck you until you're sore."

I had to admit, it sounded like a good offer. I suddenly wished we didn't live so far apart, as well. My mind wandered, thinking of the possibilities when Nathan piped up, "What's the matter, cat got your tongue?"

"No, but with an offer like that I wish I had yours between my legs right now!"

"I bet your pussy tastes gorgeous. I could lick you all day. Do you like being rimmed?"

"Can't say I've ever tried it. Into that, are you?"

"Oh yes."

It appeared the posh boy was also deliciously dirty.

"I would love to lick your tight little arsehole then stick my tongue inside and feel it twitch around me. Then when I'd got it nice and slippery, I'd stick my cock up there and ride you hard."

I couldn't deny his words were having an effect on me. I felt a heat between my thighs, almost like a blush. I suspected that if I looked in a mirror my face would be red too, and was glad he couldn't see me.

"Wow," I said, more to fill the silence than anything, "you certainly like anal play, don't you?"

"And so would you if you tried it," he replied, not missing a beat, "I've known women to squirt from anal sex alone, with no other stimulation."

"Honestly?" I was intrigued. I prided myself on my open mind, but wouldn't it hurt?

"Yes, honestly. And done properly it won't hurt a bit. Plenty of lube and even more patience is all it takes. I'd love to take your anal virginity."

I giggled. "I never thought of it like that. I certainly wouldn't say no to trying it. But I'd still want to be fucked in the traditional way, too."

"Well, you can see to that right now, can't you?"

"What do you mean?"

"You have a vibrator, don't you?"

I stifled a laugh. I did, but not in the singular. I had several toys of various shapes and sizes, but when it came to speedy and powerful orgasms, my first choice was always the same. My faithful Mr Big Rabbit Vibrator. Purchased during a special promotion on LoveHoney, it had been my favourite toy ever since, despite it costing me a fortune in batteries from its frequent use.

"I do, why?"

"I want you to wank for me, right now."

Hearing those words in his dulcet tones melted my pussy. I could, by now, feel my juices slicking up my labia and drenching my underwear. I had no objection to his demand, except to question, "And what are you going to do?"

"Stroke my cock as I listen, of course. Then envisage your face as I come. I'd love to spunk all over you, especially your ass."

"Enough with the ass. You've never even seen it."

"But I have a spectacular image in my head. Now, are you getting your toy out, or what?"

"Yes. Hang on a minute."

I rolled over on my bed, where I'd been lounging during our conversation and reached over to my bedside table. I opened the door and retrieved Mr Big. Rolling onto my back I began to wriggle out of my jeans and thong ready for some naughty time.

"What are you doing now?" Nathan enquired.

"I'm just trying to get my jeans and thong off, then I'm ready to play."

"Is that right? Has our dirty talk made you wet?"

Grinning at his confidence, I whipped off my clothes, and touched myself. I'd known I was wet, but it still surprised me to discover just how much.

"*Very* wet."

"God I wish I was there now, burying my head between your thighs and licking up all those juices, ready to slide my cock in your tight little pussy."

"Me too. But for now, I'll just have to make do with Mr Big."

As if to prove my point, I pushed the button, stirring the vibrator into life.

"Tell me exactly what you're doing."

I send Mr Big south and give Nathan a running commentary of what's happening…

"I'm rubbing the vibrator up and down my vulva, alternately teasing my clit and my labia, occasionally delving deeper so the head of the vibrator nestles against the entrance to my soaking pussy…"

I hear his breathing grow heavier on the other end of the line, so I continue, "I'm slowly pushing the vibrator inside myself. Its length and girth are stretching my pussy. I'm imagining it's you, kissing my neck and shoulders as your cock fills my hole. I'm gently twisting the fake cock, as the rim of its head stimulates my g-spot. I'm thrusting and twisting it inside me."

"Go on baby, go on. My cock is red hot and rigid. I've had to slow down before I explode."

His words just fuelled my passion further and I

ramped up the speed of the bunny ears on my clit, knowing my orgasm would soon be upon me.

"I've just turned up the speed of my vibrator so we can come together. I'm stroking my clit with the bunny ears, wishing they were your tongue and lips."

I gasp as the familiar tingles signal the onset of my climax.

"I'm opening my legs as wide as they'll go and fucking myself with the toy. I'm wishing it was you, your hips thrusting and pounding against mine, your sweat dripping from your brow onto me and my hands digging into your arse cheeks."

"I'd love for you to dig your nails into me, leaving little dents on my ass and scratch marks down the length of my back."

"I don't think I'd be able to help myself. The faster and harder you go, the more wild I become."

"Ooh, you little wildcat. Will you pull my hair and slap my face?"

"If you want me to."

"What are you doing now?"

"I'm still fucking myself. Race you to the finish line?"

"It's hardly going to be a race darling, I can barely hold back as it is. If we were doing this for real, it'd all be over by now, you make me so horny."

"That's nice to hear. I trust you'd soon be ready to go again after coming? I'm insatiable, you know."

"I don't doubt it. Come for me, sweetheart. I want to hear you."

"You can listen from close quarters then."

I moved the phone from my ear and rested my arm on my thigh, so he'd be able to hear the noise of the vibrator, and the squelching of my pussy. I continued to slide the shaft in and out of my saturated hole, knowing he could hear the movement. My urge to come grew stronger and so I concentrated on my swollen clit once more. Bringing the handset back to my ear, I said, "I'm almost there. I wish I was coming all over your face, or your prick."

"Sounds good. I'm holding out for you. Let me know, and we'll do it together."

"I'm flicking the ears across my clit like crazy now. The power is on full and I'm mega close."

The intense tingling feeling started again, growing and growing until…

"Now!" I moaned, as the waves hit and my pussy contracted crazily around the shaft of Mr Big and my entire body felt release.

Almost immediately, Nathan sucked in a huge breath.

"Mmm…" then silence.

49

I could hear my heartbeat thundering in my ears and I let the vibrator slip out of me with an audible 'plop'.

Nathan suddenly broke the silence.

"Fucking hell, that was incredible. I haven't come that hard or that much in ages. My balls are well and truly emptied."

"Glad to be of service. Imagine what it'd be like for real." I smiled.

"I don't want to imagine. I intend to find out for real, if you're willing."

"Oh I'm more than willing. I can't wait to get my hands on you."

"Nor I you, sweetheart. So, when are you free so I can give you a proper seeing to?"

Somehow, I suspected that I wouldn't be going through nearly as many batteries in the near future.

Later, on ending the call with Nathan, I immediately logged on and ordered a job lot of condoms and some other kinky things. I fully intended to ensure he was as good as his word with regards the 'proper seeing to.' I couldn't wait.

Tech Support
by Sommer Marsden

"I've done it again," I whisper into the phone. Extension eleven is lit up; Tech Support. The hot little red button that matches my wildly beating heart and the moisture in the crotch of my panties. "Can you come quickly?"

Well, not too quickly, I think and grin.

"I'll be right there, Doris," he says and I can hear the smile in his voice. For some reason, his voice reminds me of sinful dark chocolate melting on my tongue.

I wait and cross my legs. That's not good. I uncross them and swivel my seat. I bounce my knee and I wonder how long it can take him to walk down the hall. It has been an eternity since I hung up the phone. Hasn't it?

I hear the heavier walk of a man. Women swish and sway down the centre aisle all day, but when a man walks past it's different. A different vibration and different rhythm. The cubicle walls shake just a bit more when a man walks by. I hold my breath and only release it when I start to feel lightheaded.

There he is, dark hair and glasses. Brown eyes and a tired smile. He has been working overtime and the sleep deprivation is showing in the lines around his eyes. A little too heavy, a little too pale, a little too average for my normal likes. My heart kicks up into overtime and I feel my pussy clench just a bit. I am way too worked up.

I take a deep breath. "Sorry," I say softly. I am lying through my teeth. I am not sorry at all. Not one little bit. But he thinks I am and his cheeks flush with red and he smiles. He shakes his head.

"Believe it or not, I'm grateful for you, Doris. As long as you work here, I have job security." He moves into the tiny confines of my cubicle and the air grows charged around me. At least my nipples think so, because they stand at attention and rub against the warm white silk of my blouse.

"Glad I can help," I joke. I brace myself for what will come next. The top three buttons on my blouse undone, I am prepared today.

"Doris, Doris, Doris, what am I going to do with you?" Mike asks.

Fuck me? But I don't say it. I hold my breath instead and his arms go around me. He stands behind my office chair and reaches his arms around on either side of mine. There they are. His hands. On my keyboard. All the while his breath is on my neck because his head is next to mine. I can see the fluorescence reflected in his glasses as he fixes my mangled program. I was never really good with tables. They stump me. So it is not hard for me to fuck them up to earn a visit from Mike and his hands.

"You can click and drag this over here, you know?" he says and I watch him work that mouse. To me, it's like watching porn. The dark hair on his knuckles makes me weak in the knees. The way the tendons flex just below the skin. And the scar on his right index finger that looks like a crescent moon has starred in many of my fantasies. The way it would disappear as he fucked me with his fingers. The flash of white flesh dipping into my pink recesses. I shiver.

"I didn't know that," I say to prolong exposure.

"Yes, you did. I told you last time." His hot breath slides down into the vee of my blouse, caresses my cleavage.

"Oh. Oops."

"I need an admin assistant to work this project tomorrow. Can you help? Faye is busy and she's a pain in the ass anyway. I know it's Saturday but please. Can you do it?"

"Me?" I say to his middle finger. Then I tear my gaze up to his open, friendly, clueless face and say, "Sure. What time do you want me? Should I be here! What time should I be here?"

"Seven."

"I'll bring donuts for everyone," I say. He punches a few keys and I watch his big fingers dance over the tiny keys. I squeeze my inner thighs together and a warm ribbon of pleasure fills my pussy.

"What everyone? You and me, kid. Skeleton crew."

My mouth goes dry and I feel like I might faint. Go all girly and pass out and slide right out of the chair. "Oh," I manage.

"You're all fixed up." He squeezes my shoulder and the pressure from his strong hands stops my breath. "See you in the morning?"

I nod. The moment he is gone, I scamper off. Run to the small private bathroom as fast as my two-inch heels will let me. I slump against the mauve-coloured door, prop one heel on the sink and get myself off. One orgasm, two orgasms, three orgasms, like brightly coloured poppies blooming just for me.

I walk back to my desk. Cheeks flushed, heart erratic, body warm. I cannot believe I have just done that. There's no telling what I'll do tomorrow when it's just me and Mike. Nothing. Nothing at all. I will control myself and act like a pro. Mike has no interest in me. Sadly.

"I did it again," I say and stare at the red indicator on my phone. Only, this time, I really have done it and not on purpose. "I don't know what I hit. The whole thing is gone. It's gone!" My voice is going up and my eyes are tearing up. Damn.

"I'll be right there," he says and laughs. His easy laughter makes me feel worse. Here we are on a Saturday working overtime and I screwed up. I lost the document because I wasn't focused on the inventory list. I was focused on my vivid dirty movie of me and Mike. And his fingers. The way he would pinch my nipples before running his finger slowly down my chest, between my breasts, and over the flat of my belly. How my stomach would do that fluttering thing it does when something almost tickles but doesn't quite and...

"What's gone?" Mike says and stands in the doorway of my cubicle with his hands on his hips. His watch band is thick black leather, like a biker. I've never seen him in jeans. He looks completely normal and totally different.

"The spreadsheet for inventory."

He walks forward, grinning. "I doubt it's

gone."

"It is. I was typing and poof! Gone! Blank document."

Mike reaches around me. A move that should be very familiar but somehow never grows old and says right in my ear, "Just minimize it. You must have hit Control N by accident. New document. Remember?"

Now I feel stupid. But the wave of goosebumps that has gone up my neck lets me forget how stupid I feel. My nipples peak in my pink and black skull T-shirt and I am fighting the urge to squirm. We are alone. In the office. Completely. I can't seem to swallow. "Sorry." I say it so much, I should get it tattooed on me.

"I like this," he says and I notice that his voice sounds different. More assured. Deeper.

"What?"

"This T-shirt. The snaps right here –" He takes his hand off my mouse and slides one finger down into my cleavage. His finger is hot and hard and I watch it dip between my breasts and I am mesmerized.

"Thank you."

"You're welcome. But I'd like it better open," he says and tugs.

The final two silver snaps let go with a *pop! pop!*

I shift in my seat and it doesn't help. It does nothing to dampen the pulse that has started to beat steadily between my thighs. I close my eyes and focus on the inhale.

"And I like the way you look when you get all flustered. And the way your breasts move up, up, up when you are trying to get a deep breath. Like right now," he says right against my earlobe. Then he dips his head and kisses me right above my heart. His lips are warm and soft and I can smell his shampoo.

"Oh," I say, brilliantly.

His hands come back in and gather me up. Wrap around me and then tug me to my feet. I go very willingly. Like some pretty boneless thing. "I like these jeans. They are well loved," he says, hooking his hand in the front. Then he tugs and my little silver buttons give up the ghost. I am bare inside my denim and his hand slides down into my pants and covers me. He presses just his middle finger to the cleft of my sex and puts a hard pressure on my clit. I sink back against him.

Mike pushes my jeans down, but only to my knees. I go to kick them off and he steadies me with his hands. "No, leave them there."

So I do. I am bound by my own pants when he tilts me forward slightly and from behind pushes a finger into me. He adds another and my cunt flexes

57

around him, welcoming. Damn. And I can't see it.

"You can watch my fingers next time," he laughs and I feel my eyes roll back. So he does know. I smile.

I close my eyes and picture the crescent moon scar being swallowed by my red-flushed pussy. I hang my head down and the computer fan kicks on with a whir. Mike strokes me slowly until I feel that tightness start. His other index finger rests with still but firm pressure on my clit. I'm making little sounds in my throat now.

"Almost there, Doris," he says and I feel the velvet head of his cock nudge me. I push back and try to widen my stance. "No, no, nice and tight together," says Mike, pushing against my hips with his palms. Holding my legs together so tight that my knees and ankles touch. He pushes again, tilts me forward more and slides home. One finger back to my clit and he starts a slow steady stroke that accents the intense friction. The chair rolls a little and he steadies us.

He puts his finger in my mouth and I lick at it. His fingers have the heady perfume of sex and attraction. He continues to stroke and rock and I come. Easy and sharp like a firecracker going off in the summertime.

He lets me hold on to the chair now and it rolls forward until it bangs the desk. I am now stretched out like a trapeze artist, my legs still snug in my denim cocoon. "Say it for me, Doris," he says.

I don't get it. Say what? But that is mostly because my brain has gone shiny and white with endorphins and I am slow on the uptake.

He's thrusting high and hard now, panting with his eagerness. His breath fans out over my back and my nipples grow even harder as the fine hairs on my neck stand. He gives me a clue. "Tech Support," he says in his professional voice.

I'm right there again. His finger is pushing me closer to the edge. His pressure is hard. Almost too hard. Just as I like it. I get it, now.

He lets out a groan as I whisper, "I've done it again."

I come around him and Mike's loud orgasm follows close behind. He thrusts all the way until the last flicker works through me. Then he laughs and smacks my ass lightly.

"Why yes, Doris. Yes, you have. And I hope you'll do it again."

Oh, no worries there. Mike can count on me.

On the Beach
by Primula Bond

Swimming always gets me going. Blood pumping through these sluggish old veins after being holed up in the holiday cottage with a load of rutting couples. I love it when the water's cold and rough. Far out there a couple of surfers are wrestling with the waves. Here the beach is deserted.

And now I've earned a kip. The sun's really warm after the cold water. I whip my bathing suit off and flop down onto my towel but my heart's still drumming, my body still buzzing. I turn on my back, stretch my legs out, point my toes to make them look longer. Hmm, still pretty good.

A breath of air tickles my slightly parted fanny. I open my legs a little more. I grope about in the sand to find my oil, but I can't find it. My hand flops back onto my bare stomach and the touch electrifies me. I move my fingertips down to the hairless groove running along the top of my thigh and that makes me jump, too. The skin is the largest organ of the human body, and boy is it the most sensitive.

There's another place, though. So sensitive it could make me come with a butterfly kiss. My hand wanders back up to my breast, just brushes the top, avoiding the nipples. They swell out luxuriantly. My stomach flutters.

I drop my hands. Is it possible to tease yourself? The sun rests on my eyelids while my hand drags back to my stomach. I move it in circles, frantic messages puckering up my nipples. My stomach tightens. My thighs fidget on the towel, open up wider. I fan my fingers, catching at a hardening nipple, and sidle the other hand downwards to the warm nest of hair. My fingers tangle in the wet curls, pulling strands, feeling each hair tug on the tender skin.

My middle finger extends down the crack and I half gasp, half giggle at the moist blood-heat warmth just inside the lips. That's not just damp from the sea although I wonder what it would taste like now. I wiggle my finger, feeling the sliver of sensitive flesh. I shock it into tingling response. I moan softly, sure that the sound is only in my ears.

A shadow crosses my face and I swear, thinking a cloud is obscuring the sun. But it's too solid for that. There's a tall shape a couple of feet away. Surely not the others, come to spy on me from the cottage? I raise myself up on my elbow, ready to give them hell. My breast bounces against my arm. I raise one knee to get myself upright and a droplet of juice runs out of my crack and across my thigh.

It's not my friends. It's one of the surfers. His short wetsuit is rolled down his torso and he has his back to the sea. He can see me clearly, but I'm half blinded by the glare. I raise one hand to shield my eyes and take a good look at him. Sex on legs. Like something out of a beer advert. He's lithe and tanned. His face is young. So young. Tiny gold prickles of barely shaved stubble speckle his brown cheeks. Hectic flushes of blood are just visible under the skin. Is he blushing?

I try to remember myself at his age. It wasn't so long ago, for God's sake. He's seventeen, eighteen. Maybe nineteen. Definitely a boy and yet his body has been worked on. Hard. No ounce of puppy fat. His arms are big with muscle.

I let my eyes flutter back to his face. I open my mouth to speak, but he's not about to make small talk. His bright blue eyes are fixed on my big breasts, hanging there in the sunshine. I must look like some kind of nude sculpture there on the towel. I suppose I could always pretend I'm one of those naturists.

But the naturists always claim there's nothing sexual about nakedness, don't they? What bollocks. I reckon this boy's nakedness would be a blatant invitation to a shag-fest. His eyes are burning on me and my nipples harden as if agreeing with my assessment. They shrink into tight little arrowheads. Pointing directly at my young stranger.

The young man/boy swallows, getting the message. He scuffles his bare feet in the sand. Shit. He's trying to get away. I want to stretch out and stop him. But no. He's just planting them more firmly in that kind of swaggering stance young men have. Through his tight wet suit I can see his groin bulging against the black cloth. I want to rip it off here and now. I want to know what's going on underneath.

'Surf up today?' I suddenly ask into the sizzling silence. I can imagine my mates up at the cottage giggling at my lousy attempt at surf-speak. 'I thought there were two of you out there.'

He nods, and tosses his head back towards the waves. His hair is beginning to dry into bleached strands.

'My brother's still out there. I got a cramp.'

'I can see that.'

The fluttering in my stomach is back with a vengeance. No, forget fluttering. Nothing lady-like about this sensation. It's twisting and tightening with total lust. I can't believe I'm still sprawled here like some kind of centrefold. Usually I would have lifted the towel by now to cover myself up. I'd have made some shy, dismissive remark to send him on his way, but right now his glowing stare and his unmistakeable hard-on are just too good to waste. I'm not letting this opportunity pass. Apart from anything else, I intend to dine out on it tonight. The others will never believe me.

'Want some lemonade?' God, I sound like his aunt.

'My dad says you should never accept drinks from strangers,' he croaks with a lopsided grin, and I laugh. How sexy is that grin? How sexy is it that we're strangers? I take the bottle from the cool bag and wave it at him.

'I say you're big enough to look after yourself.' I'm still laughing. I pat the towel beside me. He steps closer. I'm making him feel safe. He leans across me, and swigs from the bottle. 'So,' I go on, my voice husky with laughter and desire. 'Do you know this part of Devon?'

'No. It's my first time.'

Colour floods his cheeks even more as he says it, and this time I rein in my dirty chuckle. I quietly take the lemonade from him, keeping my green eyes calmly on his burning blue ones, and without wiping his spittle off the neck of the bottle I flick my tongue round the wet rim before tilting my head back to take a deep swallow. Now his eyes are on my throat as the cold liquid swishes down. This is like something out of a movie.

'I mean, it's the first time we've been down to this coast,' he stammers. 'Dad's rented a place for the summer. He insisted we come here this year. Normally we go to Constantine Bay, in Cornwall. The surf's miles better over there. So's the surfing crowd. I mean, it's just dead round here, isn't it?'

'That depends what you're after,' I remark lazily. The bottle is still hovering above my open mouth as if I'm about to give it head. I lick it again, turning myself on with the suggestive swipe of my tongue. Then I wrap my lips round the long cool shape and swallow a little more. His Adam's apple jumps. I screw the top back on. On an impulse I put the bottle not back in the cool bag but between my legs, resting it up against my pussy. I can't stifle a gasp as the cold plastic meets the sensitive, warm flesh. I lean back, letting it rest there, restraining myself from grabbing it and rubbing it up and down my hot slit like a sex toy. The urge won't go away. But then, nor will the boy. My voice comes out in a low moan. 'There's plenty to entertain you if you know where to look.'

'I'm beginning to realise that–'

Without the bottle the boy doesn't know what to do with his hands. So he starts rolling the wetsuit back up his stomach.

'It's too nice out here today to cover yourself up. It may not be the Med, but this lovely weather has got to be a record for Devon. Sit down for a moment. Like you said, there's nothing to do round here. So there's no rush, is there?'

'No rush,' he echoes, and his young voice dips violently into a deep manly timbre, at odds with his adolescent face. My cunt gives a couple of uncontrollably cheeky twitches, practically nudging the bottle away as I watch him wrestle with the twin urges to come and sit near me or to stand there and remain cool.

Time to be a little less obvious. I relent and draw my legs up, so that my pussy is temporarily hidden from his confused, hungry gaze, but the movement brings the bottle harder against me, its long shape pushing between my sex lips and nudging the tiny bud of my clit. I grip it with my legs and feel the droplets of condensation mingling with my own sweat and moisture.

I'm getting breathless again, as if I was still swimming. I want to show the boy what I can do with the bottle, but it's too soon. I hitch myself up the towel, pulling my shoulders back in an effort to look more sophisticated, but that just thrusts my breasts out so that his baby-blue eyes, which are still struggling to remain politely focused on my face, swivel back to watch the tightening of my red nipples.

'It may be a bit quiet, but where else can you get quite so close to nature, after the city smoke? I expect that's what your dad was after,' I whisper, trying not to giggle out loud with delight. Something is still warning me to act very calm, sit very still so as not to alarm him. 'That's why I'm stretched out here, starkers. Never do that in London, do you? Hope you don't mind me being topless like this?'

He shakes his head violently, like a little boy trying not to tell a lie, and at last, like an animal tempted in from the wild, he squats down, just by my feet. He rubs the salty strands of yellow hair off his hot face.

'So. You here on holiday, or what?'

He's giving in. He can't take his eyes off my tits, even though he's attempting to make conversation. I know my nipples are harder and darker now and impossible to ignore. Neither of us really wants to talk, do we? It's as if he's in a sweet shop with no pocket money. His tongue slides across his white teeth and he gulps. I keep my smile faint but encouraging.

'It's a mixture,' I answer. 'Work, and play.'

'So which is this bit? Work, or play?'

A soft wind comes off the sea and ruffles his

hair. He swipes it impatiently out of his eyes. My own hair tickles my face, and the wind caresses my bare skin like delicate fingers.

'Oh, that's easy. Play,' I whisper, not sure if he can hear. 'This bit is definitely play.'

I tilt forwards on to my knees, the bottle still clamped there. I pause for a moment as he blinks, focusing on the big tits bouncing right there in front of him as if they were ice creams on offer. Then I pick up one of his large hands from where it's digging frantically about in the sand. I lift it like it's a warm animal and place it on one swollen breast. My nipple spikes against his palm. His mouth drops open. My head falls back as his fingers close harder, making it ache. I spread my knees a little to balance more comfortably in front of him, dislodging the bottle. I lean back on the towel so that my spine is arched and my breasts are pushing at him, jumping up with each heartbeat.

The dry grass rustles in the slight breeze, and far away the waves curl with a collective sigh onto the beach. Both the boy and me are panting. My tits disappear into his hesitant fingers. His blue eyes blaze with a crazy request. Christ, it's enough to make me melt. Of *course* you have permission, my precious. I'm practically *begging you!*

My head feels heavy. The only energy is fizzing between my legs. I'm ready to let him take and thrust and pummel. I want to make him into a man. I have privacy, sunshine, a boy with the body of a god waiting for me to show him the way. And all the time in the world.

Lust is eating me up. His fingers dig into my breasts, wander across them and squeeze them, push them together, letting them fall, playing with them, staring at the rigid raspberry nipples. Then I kneel up and place my hands on his shoulders and push my tits into his eager face. I want him to nuzzle in, I want him to lick, suck, bite. Yes. I can tell he's never seen anyone as luscious as me. A real woman. I want this to be what he'll write home about, remember for ever. I want to smother him. He buries his face between my breasts, pressing them into his cheeks. Then he draws back. I cup one breast and offer it. I rub its taut dark nipple across his mouth. His tongue flicks out tentatively. My knees wobble and I clutch more firmly to his shoulders. My tit is angled right into his mouth.

He licks the nipple again, and his hands squeeze my breasts until they sing with delicious pain. Hands that a few minutes ago had been wrestling with a surfboard. Then his soft lips nibble up the little nub of the nipple, the tongue laps round it. He draws the burning bud into his mouth, pulling hard on it, and begins to suck. I cradle his bleached blond head, the salt water dried in granules and flecked white across his cheek bones. I could stay like this forever. His sucking makes my whole body ripple with desire.

I look away over his head, across the dunes and over the ocean, distancing myself, seeing us like a movie or a photograph, but his mouth, his teeth, keep pulling at the aching nipple and pulling me back. Electrical currents streak from my nipples to my empty, waiting cunt.

He has the other breast up by his face now. He's turning from one to the other, lapping and sucking, snuffling through his nose to breathe, groaning, biting and kneading harder and harder as if he owns my breasts. It's never enough to suck just one. They both have to be stimulated, and, boy, is he getting the hang of it. God, it's going to be earth-shattering when I get him inside me.

He's rougher, more ferocious, already more confident. I grind against him, daring him, searching for more pain to communicate more pleasure. I plant my knees on either side of his so that I'm straddling him, and still have his head crushed between my tits. I push him backwards so that, still sucking on my nipples, he's lowered onto the sand. Now I'm on top of him, my tits dangling down like heavy fruit dented by his brown fingers. I tilt my pussy towards his groin and rub against

70

his wet suit. The rough material is glorious, grating on my skin.

And I can feel the length of his dick. Still pushing my tits in his face, don't ever want him to stop, I grab at the wet suit and start to roll it off him like a second skin. He raises his hips obligingly. So sweet. He does that so eagerly and readily. Does he realise how big his fucking gorgeous erection is? I yank everything down and his cock thumps free, juddering out from the rough tangle of blond curls, pulsating golden brown like the rest of him. God, it's a work of art. Its surface is smooth like velvet, the mauve plum emerging from the soft foreskin which wrinkles back to show itself all gleaming. This gorgeous cock thumps into my hand. Now it's my turn to fold my fingers round something, and as I do it he bites my nipple so hard that I scream out with delight. I lean over him.

'Just take a little break. Try something new,' I whisper, both to myself and to him. I start to wriggle back down his body so that his head follows for a moment, still attached to my nipples. Then he falls back as I slither down towards his groin and he can only grab at my wet hair. I reach his dick, standing up like a beacon. The tip is already beading in anticipation. A fresh stick of rock.

71

I open my mouth and draw his cock into it, using my teeth as well as my tongue, draw it all in until the boy's knob knocks at the back of my throat.

He makes a sound, exquisitely shocked. His buttocks clench as I suck on him, nibbling down to the base of his shaft and licking and sucking the sweet length of it. He starts to buck about, groaning in amazement. I wonder if any of his pert little girlfriends give head like this. I doubt it. After all, I didn't have much of a clue at this age. I want him to think he's died and gone to heaven. Any minute now I'm going to heaven, too.

As I suck, I rub my tits and pussy up and down his legs. He pulls at my hair. I have to slow myself down, because we'll both come too soon. I don't want to waste this golden moment by coming all over his shinbone. My pussy is clenching frantically now. I'm leaving slicks of juice all over him.

I give his dick one last, long suck, pulling it towards my throat and nipping it with my teeth, then I let it slide along my tongue, out through my nipping teeth. Greedily I clamber back on top of him as he struggles up, seeking out my tits. I press him down on his back, tilting myself over him. We've moved some way from the towel now.

'See how beautiful it is,' I croon at him,

showing him the length of his shaft encircled by my fingers. 'See how well it's going to fit.'

I smile as I raise myself on my knees and aim the tip of his cock towards the warm hole hidden in my soft bush. I let it rest there, at the opening, just like I did with the lemonade bottle, just nudging it past my wet sex lips. I wait. I smile again, lowering myself a little more, gasping as each inch goes in. I reach under him to cup his balls in one hand and he groans again.

This tension is ecstasy, but I can't hold on to it for much longer, and slowly, luxuriously, I let the boy's knob slide up inside, all the way to the hilt. It's so tempting to ram it, let our hips start jerking, but once it's right in I force myself to pull away again. He frowns, perhaps thinking I'm rejecting him, but I just ease myself down again, moaning and tossing my head back, and the next time I do that he's with me, learning fast, pulling his own hips back, waiting when I wait.

I sigh out with the joy of being fucked by something so big and hard after months of sitting on the sidelines. As I bend over to let my tits swing across his mouth again, his eyes flip sideways and his face freezes. His hands jam onto my hips and hold me still. I don't move. I don't want to. But I see another shadow falling across his face.

'Oh, piss off, guys!' I shout, without looking

round. 'Go back to your poker game!'

'I wouldn't dream of it! This looks like a hell of a lot more fun than poker!'

A male voice, very similar to my boy's, speaks from somewhere above and behind us. I go hot and cold. I try to read the boy's expression. Then there's the unzipping sound of another wet suit, and the boy's eyes widen. First he shakes his head furiously, and then a filthy grin spreads across his face. Not a grin I've seen before. He looks at me in a different way. Kind of domineering. I'm thrown off balance. Already he's learning. Glancing at the newcomer, the boy knocks my breasts from side to side.

'My older brother,' he croaks. 'Back from the surf.'

He pulls me forwards, jamming my tits into his mouth again, and now my backside is up in the air. I want to protest but I can't move. My butt is all exposed, bouncing in front of his brother, but so gorgeous is the feel of my boy's almost aggressive mouth sucking on my sore nipples that I can't stop him. As first one nipple then the other grinds into his mouth I automatically start up the rhythm again. I'm acutely aware of my new audience. It's unutterably sexy to be watched.

I slide up and down his cock, showing off now. My muscles tighten each time to grab hold and keep him inside, and his cock is hardening even more with each thrust.

I'm just poised to ram down onto him harder than ever when my butt cheeks are pulled apart and another male body presses up against my back.

'Can't let you have all the fun, bruv,' says the voice. 'Reckon I want a go.'

'You've got some catching up to do, mate. Bloody well wait your turn.'

The first boy pulls me harder down on top of him, ramming me right up inside.

'You don't mind me watching, do you?' his brother murmurs in my ear, still fondling my buttocks.

'No,' I puff, barely able to speak. 'Don't mind.'

There's something else going on here, too. I can recognize sibling rivalry when I see it, or rather sense it. It's not that different from the 'friendly' rivalry between me and my mates up at the cottage. Our parlour games are never going to be the same after this.

I'm dizzy now, knowing I'm being watched. Who knows? Maybe the crowd up at the cottage will be down any minute, join the audience. See me in a whole new light. I gyrate as if dancing on the boy's pole, flinging myself wildly about. The urge for satisfaction and the loss of control starts to overwhelm me.

The invisible brother is right behind me, touching me everywhere. I fall onto the rigid cock inside me and the orgasm is gathering. My moans are snatched into the sea air as I rock frantically. My boy can't hold back and it's spurting out of him and I'm bucking in my own orgasm.

'Can't let you corrupt my little brother and get away with it,' the older brother says, pulling us apart. 'Reckon you need teaching, too.'

He parts my legs, gets his own cock out. I try not to smile too greedily as we all lie on the sand while the tide encroaches up the beach and the seagulls wonder what the *fuck* these tourists are up to.

Open-Bottle Policy
by Jeremy Edwards

'Well, it looks like you'll be making out on the leftovers, Dave,' said Charles with an affable smirk, as he suavely – and generously – grabbed the bill from our server.

I studied the lovely form of the woman who had waited on us, as she headed back to the kitchen. If my memory was correct, she had introduced herself as Becky. But I wasn't at all sure on this point. I'm usually pretty good with names, but not when distracted by a pair of kind, laughing eyes situated in an elegantly-impish feminine face.

Whatever her name was, I had enjoyed our brief moments of interaction this evening even more than I'd enjoyed the company of my old friends Charles and Amanda.

I assessed the appealing remnants of the exquisite Thai-fusion dinner, which all of us were now too full to dally with any further. 'What do you mean?' I said to Charles. 'You and Amanda should take some of it.' I shifted my gaze to Charles's wife. 'You'd like that, wouldn't you, Amanda?'

My friend Amanda is the type of woman who has a subtle, but potent, sexiness. I think the only reason I don't respond to her more strongly is that I'm so conscious of the fact that she's a long-time crony who's happily married to another long-time crony. It's true that I have, on occasion, fantasized about her. This sort of thing can't be helped sometimes in one's bed late at night. But under normal circumstances I have succeeded in feeling only a chummy affection for Amanda. And yet, in a tangential way, spending an hour in the presence of her charm and beauty – always well-presented in the perfect clothes and perfumes – usually leaves me in a sexy mood even if the feelings are not directed toward her.

Amanda smiled graciously. 'Charles is right, Davey. We're heading straight to the theatre from here, and we can scarcely carry big, fragrant leftover containers into the auditorium with us.'

'It wouldn't be polite, since there's not enough to share with everyone else in the audience,' added Charles.

I chuckled and nodded, recognizing that their offer of all the food was as practical as it was polite. Since my hotel room was in this very building – and equipped with both a refrigerator and a microwave – it was logical that the leftovers would devolve to me.

'Sorry again that we couldn't get you a ticket,' said Charles. 'Next time you're coming to town, give us a little more notice!' He gave me a playful punch in the arm.

I laughed. 'If my company ever gives *me* more notice, I promise I'll give *you* more notice.'

'Oh – what about all this wine?' said Amanda suddenly.

We had ordered a modest-looking Merlot that had turned out to be remarkably good. In the course of this convivial but all-too-brief dinner, Charles and I had consumed only one glass apiece, and Amanda had limited herself to half a glass. None of us wanted to see what was left in the bottle go back to the kitchen – though, for my part, I wouldn't have objected to watching Becky *carry* it back to the kitchen, if you know what I mean.

'Dave can take that, too,' Charles answered.

'Can I?' I wondered aloud. 'Aren't there rules against it?'

'Let's ask the server,' Charles replied optimistically. 'After all, you wouldn't even be taking it out of the building.' At that instant Becky reappeared, and Charles gave a jovial wave to attract her back to our table.

'All ready?' Becky asked. I observed that although it was Charles who was proffering his credit card, and Charles who had requested her return, her eyes kept shifting in my direction. Or was I just imagining this, because I found her so pretty?

'Question,' Charles began. 'Can Dave here take the rest of the wine up to his room in your hotel?'

Now Becky turned her gaze fully toward me, and her mouth curled into a mischievous smile. 'So, Dave wants all the wine, eh?'

I probably blushed. 'I guess I do. That is, I'd be glad to share it... if I had someone to share it with. But seeing as I'm all alone in this great big hotel, I'm fairly sure I can do justice to what's left in the bottle.' I thought I saw something especially gentle creep into Becky's smile as I said the word 'alone'.

'There's no rule against that, is there?' Charles continued.

'Actually,' said Becky with a professional briskness, 'there *is* an ordinance about open bottles in this town. But since Dave isn't exactly leaving the premises, it may be okay. Let me ask the manager.' Watching Becky's confident behind walk toward the manager's station, I thought about how she seemed to enjoy calling me by name, as if we were already pals.

As Becky led him our way, her boss telegraphed his accommodating answer by means of a wide, customer-service-friendly grin. 'You'd like to take the wine upstairs?' He was looking at Charles and Amanda, but Becky nudged his elbow and cocked her head my way.

'If it's no problem,' I said.

'No, there won't be a problem with that,' said the manager. 'Our open-bottle policy within the building merely states that your server must escort you to the elevator. We simply need to verify that you are taking the bottle directly to your hotel room, you understand.' He flashed us another cordial grin, then retreated.

Becky beamed. 'I'll get the cork, and then I can see you out whenever you're ready, Dave. And I'll be back in a sec with your credit card, sir.' I saw that she barely acknowledged Charles, even as she addressed him. Her attention seemed to be locked in on the co-ordinates of my face.

A minute later, the leftovers had been boxed, the wine had been re-corked, the credit card slip had been signed, and Amanda was telling Becky, course by course, how much we'd all relished the meal.

'I'll let my manager know that I'm taking you to the elevator now,' Becky said to me when

81

Amanda had finished. 'I'm due to go on my dinner break, anyway,' she confided before leaving us.

'Well, buddy, it looks like you're in good hands,' said Charles with a wink. Beautiful Amanda tittered conspiratorially, while favouring me with a goodbye kiss on the cheek.

'Enjoy the show!' I shouted as they left the restaurant.

I didn't realize that Becky had managed to sneak up behind me, and I nearly jumped when I heard her perky 'All set, Dave?'

'Huh? Oh – yeah, I guess so.'

She touched my elbow and steered me toward the door. I was wearing short sleeves, and the feel of her fingers on my skin sent a thrill through me.

It took us only a few seconds to cross the lobby to the elevator, but the car was currently occupied somewhere above. Becky, carrying out her professional assignment, continued to hold the wine bottle while we waited.

'This feels so silly,' she suddenly blurted, with a rather unprofessional giggle that I found adorable. 'Almost like we're on a date, or something.' Then she added earnestly, 'Not that dates are silly, mind you.'

Her presence was making me feel like I was melting all over. Well, almost all over – there was one place on my anatomy where I was, by contrast, definitely solidifying.

The elevator arrived. I saw that this was the time to act.

'Hadn't you better escort me all the way upstairs?' I said with a transparent slyness. 'I wouldn't want you to get in trouble with your boss for not *ensuring* that the wine went straight to my room.'

Becky looked at me, looked back toward the restaurant, and then back at me again. She didn't say anything, but her eyes glinted. I was holding the elevator door open, and she entered swiftly.

While the car ascended with a soothing whir, Becky broke the silence. 'I don't know if this was strictly necessary, according to the open-bottle rules. But I *am* going on a break... and I can do whatever I like on my break.' She stepped closer to me. 'Whatever I like,' she repeated. And she reached forward and tapped my chest, ever so briefly.

I looked at Becky and took in all I could see. Bright blonde hair, long and casual. Those laughing eyes, that sensitive mouth. The trim, athletic body, shown off to nice effect in her white blouse and tight black slacks. I felt warm, nervous... and excited.

The spell was broken for a moment by the 'ding' of the elevator, and the door opened on to my floor. Becky stepped out without hesitation, in perfect stride with me. As I led the way along the corridor, she hummed cheerfully. The cozy sound of our feet shuffling along the carpet accompanied her voice very nicely.

'Here we are,' I said when we'd arrived at my door. I stood at the threshold, brimming with desire and uncertainty.

'Aren't you going to open it?' she coaxed.

So I opened it. She entered, ahead of me, wine bottle still in hand. Hoping for the best, I closed the door behind us.

Once inside the room, I quickly put the leftovers down, not even giving much thought to where. Becky finally handed over the bottle.

'Thank you,' I said self-consciously. There was a short silence while I decided what to say next. 'Would you like some wine?' was what I came up with.

'Thanks for the offer,' she replied. 'But it wouldn't be appropriate for me to return to work with alcohol in my system.'

'Ah, of course,' I said. 'I'm so sorry.'

She reclaimed the bottle from me and placed it out of the way, on a table. 'Don't be sorry,' she said. 'There are plenty of other things we can do during my break.'

'We?' I barely had time to utter it before she

began to smother me with kisses, while reaching around to grab my butt in her strong little hands.

Because her restaurant provided room service, it was natural that Becky would be familiar with the standard layout of rooms in the hotel. So I was delighted, but not surprised, that she was able to navigate us toward the bed without even having to watch where she was going.

'Just because that bottle's sealed, it doesn't mean everything around here has to stay under wraps,' she breathed in my ear. An instant later, I felt her reach for my zipper, and I reciprocated by teasing hers out of its home in the nook of her sexy trousers. We wiggled the clothing down each other's legs with semi-graceful synchronization, engaging in an eager dance of undressing.

The dance continued as Becky lifted my cock out of my shorts, and I stroked the moist black cotton between her legs.

'I can't wait,' she chirped, rushing to slide her own panties down while my prick stayed in a holding pattern. Then she sank into the bed, giggling becomingly and spreading her nicely-toned thighs so that I could see her soft blonde curls and her glistening wetness. Her blouse was still buttoned; nevertheless, as I pounced on her I felt the warmth of her breasts, reaching me through bra and blouse and my own shirt.

Her sensuous wiggling beckoned my face down to her centre of pleasure. I kissed and licked at her sweetness, and she squealed and pressed herself against my mouth. Despite the sturdy vigour of her personality, she felt delicate down here – and she tasted, indeed, like a delicacy.

Becky was ready to be brought to ecstasy, and it was no challenge to do so. Her muscular legs kicked beautifully as she climaxed.

'You certainly know how to get things flowing,' she purred, lifting my head. 'Now, how about we put a cork in it for a while?'

She guided my cock into her vessel, and I felt the warmth of her love-vintage bathing and caressing me.

Friendly little kisses and nibbles – signs of a healthy appetite – pampered my neck and ears while we bounced together. All too soon, I felt myself spilling into her, and she clutched me tightly and whispered my name.

'Oh, Becky…' I answered.

She guffawed, and hugged me even tighter. 'It's *Betsy*.'

She rolled me over, and straddled me like a woman who knows exactly what she wants to get out of her dinner break. Then she proceeded to show me, in no uncertain terms, that she wouldn't dream of holding an innocent mistake against me.

With my prick in the spirited embrace of Betsy's powerful cunt, my mind rolled hither and yon in ecstasy, and random thoughts about the evening began to flash by. Charles had been right about taking the wine upstairs, said one random thought. And he'd been right that I was in good hands, said another.

By now, Betsy was fucking me with a positively athletic exuberance, and leading us rapidly toward a joint climax. As our bodies vibrated together, I heard something crackle from behind my shoulders. Styrofoam. *Oops.*

Charles had been right again. I *was* making out on the leftovers!

Looking for love? Our unique dating sites offer the perfect way to meet someone who shares your fantasies.

www.xcitedating.com
Find someone who'll turn fiction into reality and make your fantasies come true.

www.xcitespanking.com
Spanking is our most popular theme – here's the place to find out why!

www.girlfun-dating.co.uk
Lesbian dating for girls who wanna have fun!

www.ultimatecurves.com
For sexy, curvy girls and the men who love them.

Also available at £2.99

Confessions Volume 2

Some experiences just have to be
confessed!

There's a knack to getting two girls into
bed at the same time. Three simple
rules, and one man tells you how ...
A guy whose interest was taboo reveals
that he never had trouble recruiting
willing female lovers, especially in
underground settings ...
Over the knee and on the bare; here's a
confession to a lifetime indulging a
spanking obsession ...
Even the cruellest of teases eventually
offers a taste of the rarest fruit; the
trick is to learn how to watch and wait
until her desire is ripe ...

ISBN 9781907016325

For more information and great offers
please visit
www.xcitebooks.com